llama llama misses mama

Anna Dewdney

W9-BDF-758

VIKING

llama llama misses mama

Anna Dewdney

VIKING

Llama Llama, warm in bed.
Wakey, wakey, sleepyhead!

Llama school begins **today!**
Time to learn and time to play!

Make the bed and
find some clothes.

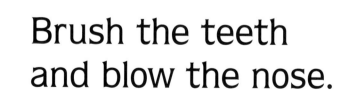

Brush the teeth
and blow the nose.

Eat some breakfast.
Clean the plate.

Whoops!
Oh my—
we're running late!

Drive to school
and park the car.

Tell the teacher
who you are.

Meet new faces.
Hear new names.
See new places.
Watch new games.

Hang the coat
and say good-bye.

Llama Llama
feeling shy. . . .

Mama Llama goes away.
Llama Llama has to stay.

Strange new teacher.
Strange new toys.
Lots of kids
and lots of noise!

What would Llama like to do?
Llama Llama feels so new. . . .

Build a castle out of blocks?
Make a rocket from a box?
Llama Llama shakes his head.
Llama walks away instead.

Here's a little chugga-choo
with a captain and a crew.
Would the llama like a ride?
Llama Llama tries to hide.

Reading stories on the rug.
Kids are cuddled, sitting snug.

Would the llama like to look?

Llama Llama
hates that book.

Time for lunch! Now find a seat.

Llama doesn't want to eat.
Llama makes a little moan.
Llama Llama feels **alone.**

Llama misses Mama so. . . .

Why did Mama Llama **go?**

It's too much
for little Llama . . .

Llama Llama MISSES MAMA!

Don't be sad, new little llama!
It's OK to miss your mama.
But don't forget—
when day is through,

she will come **right back** to you.

Llama Llama, please don't fuss.
Have some fun and play with **us!**

Put on coats and run outside.
See the playhouse! Try the slide.

Tag and jump rope. Hide and seek.
Close your eyes and do not peek!

Now it's time to
draw and write.
Great big crayons.
Colors bright.

Take some paper
from the stack . . .

Teacher gets a
good-bye hug.

Wave to friends on reading rug.

Climb the playhouse with the slide.
See if Mama fits inside.

Lots to show and lots to say!
Back again another day. . . .

Llama finds out something new—

He loves Mama . . .

and **SCHOOL**, too!

For Berol, my first to go off to school

VIKING

Published by Penguin Group

Penguin Young Readers Group, 345 Hudson Street, New York, New York 10014, U.S.A.

Penguin Group (Canada), 90 Eglinton Avenue East, Suite 700, Toronto, Ontario, Canada M4P 2Y3 (a division of Pearson Penguin Canada Inc.)

Penguin Books Ltd, 80 Strand, London WC2R 0RL, England

Penguin Books Ltd, Registered Offices: 80 Strand, London WC2R 0RL, England

First published in 2009 by Viking, a division of Penguin Young Readers Group

3 5 7 9 10 8 6 4 2

Copyright © Anna Dewdney, 2009

All rights reserved

LIBRARY OF CONGRESS CATALOGING-IN-PUBLICATION DATA

Dewdney, Anna.

Llama Llama misses Mama / by Anna Dewdney.

p. cm.

Summary: Llama Llama experiences separation anxiety on his first day of nursery school.

ISBN 978-0-670-06198-3 (hardcover)

Special Markets ISBN 978-0-670-01269-5 Not for resale

[1. Stories in rhyme. 2. Separation anxiety—Fiction. 3. Nursery schools—Fiction. 4. Schools—Fiction. 5. Llamas—Fiction.] I. Title.

PZ8.3.D498Lkt 2009

[E]—dc22

2008037451

Manufactured in China

Set in ITC Quorum

This Imagination Library edition is published by Penguin Group (USA), a Pearson company, exclusively for Dolly Parton's Imagination Library, a not-for-profit program designed to inspire a love of reading and learning, sponsored in part by The Dollywood Foundation. Penguin's trade editions of this work are available wherever books are sold.